Alexa Tewkesbury

CWR

See back of book for list of National Distributors.
Unless otherwise indicated, all Scripture references are from the
Good News Bible, copyright © American Bible Society 1966, 1971,
1976, 1992, 1994.
Concept development, editing, design and production by CWR
Printed in Finland by Bookwell
ISBN: 978-1-85345-596-4

Hi! We're the Topz Gang

– Topz because we all live at the 'top' of something ... either in houses at the top of the hill, at the top of the flats by the park, even sleeping in a top bunk counts! We are all Christians, and we go to Holly Hill School.

We love Jesus, and try to work out our faith in God in everything we do – at home, at school and with our friends. That even means trying to show God's love to the Dixons Gang who tend to be bullies, and can be a real pain!

If you'd like to know more about us, visit our website at **www.cwr.org.uk/topz** You can read all about us, and how you can get to know and understand the Bible more by reading our *Topz* notes, which are great fun, and written every two months just for you!

BOYS ONLY

This book is the private property of:

_____

(So if you're not me, why are you reading it??)

Age:
My birthday (tick a box):

☐ Been and gone this year   ☐ Coming soon

☐ Ages away   ☐ Can't remember

I look like this:
(Draw yourself here)

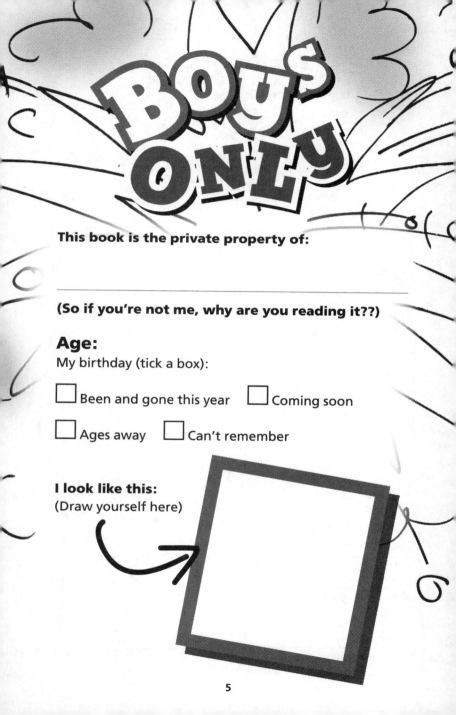

Family Stuff

How big is your family?

Number of brothers _____

Number of sisters _____

None of the above _____

Are there any pets in your family?

If **YES**, draw them here and write their names.
If **NO**, draw a pet you'd like to have and give it a name:

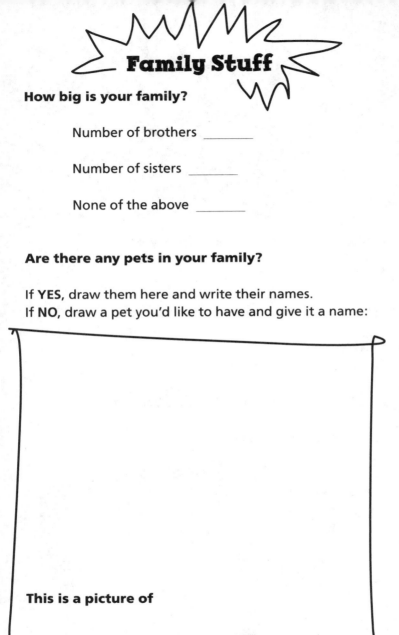

This is a picture of

_____

Benny's Potty Pets!

Benny doesn't have any pets but would love one of these:

elephant
pig
skunk
crab
owl

wolf
tarantula
bear
porcupine
badger

Can you find them in the word search?

S	Z	H	X	X	D	S	K	M	R	T	A
K	E	F	L	O	W	P	E	R	N	L	E
U	A	L	V	G	O	K	M	J	U	Q	L
N	R	T	E	N	P	V	R	T	T	C	G
K	H	L	G	P	K	V	N	H	R	P	V
B	R	E	I	J	H	A	M	A	N	X	G
X	H	A	P	R	R	A	B	X	D	B	Y
I	H	M	E	A	P	A	N	H	K	I	T
B	X	N	T	B	D	U	H	T	B	U	N
C	P	M	B	G	W	Y	V	G	L	J	M
U	N	H	E	R	C	F	B	J	W	Y	D
P	O	R	C	U	P	I	N	E	O	C	V

Answers on page 110

Six of the Best

Paul loves being in the Topz Gang. Unmuddle the
letters of each name below to make a list of his TOPZ
six best friends:

hnjo   _ _ _ _

sjeoi   _ _ _ _ _

nynbe   _ _ _ _ _

edva   _ _ _ _

rhaas   _ _ _ _ _

ydnan   _ _ _ _ _

Write down the names of six of your best friends:

_____

_____

_____

_____

_____

_____

Draw yourself with your six friends here:

Who wants to be everyone's BEST FRIEND so that He can love and care for us?

→ **G** _ _

School Stuff

The Topz Gang moan and groan about school sometimes, but they love it really – especially as it means they can see each other most days. How about you? What can you tell Topz about YOUR school and what you do there?

Draw your school uniform here

Things I like about school

_____

_____

_____

_____

_____

_____

_____

_____

Things I would definitely change about school

_____

_____

_____

_____

_____

_____

_____

_____

I love writing stories but I don't like school dinners!

School Stuff (continued)

**Have you ever been in a play
at your school?**   Yes ☐ No ☐

If yes, what was it called?

_____

Was it a musical?   Yes ☐ No ☐

What part did you play?

_____

**What did your costume look like? Can you draw
yourself wearing it – or one you would like to
wear – here?**

Do you ever go on school trips?
If yes, where have you been?

_____

How do you get to and from school?

☐ Walk   ☐ Bus

☐ Boat   ☐ Rickshaw

☐ Car   ☐ Train

☐ Helicopter   ☐ Bicycle

Teacher: Why are you late, Joseph?

Joseph: Because of a sign down the road.

Teacher: What does a sign have to do with your being late?

Joseph: The sign said, 'School Ahead, Go Slow!'

When You Grow Up (1) ...

How TALL would you like to be (tick a box)?

Extremely TALL ☐

Quite TALL ☐

A bit TALL ☐

Not very TALL at all ☐

How tall are you now?
Write your height and the date you were measured here:

I am _____ on _____ / _____ / _____

I would like to be tall because

_____

OR
I don't mind whether I'm tall or not because

_____

GUESS WHAT ...?
The tallest man in history
is said to have measured
an UNBELIEVABLE
2.72 metres (8 feet
11.1 inches)!

14

Tall and Small in the Bible

The book of 1 Samuel, chapter 17 in the Old Testament part of the Bible tells us about a very TALL man. His name was GOLIATH. He didn't want to make friends with God and was an enemy of His people. So, however much He loved him, God couldn't be Goliath's friend either.

There are small people in the Bible, too. In the New Testament, the book of Luke (chapter 19 verses 1–10) tells the story of a very small man. He wasn't at all popular. People didn't like him because he used to steal their money. But even though he did bad things, the man still wanted to catch a glimpse of Jesus – and being small wasn't going to stop him. When Jesus arrived in his town one day, the small man climbed up a very tall tree to make sure he could see Him over the heads of the crowds who'd come to see Him, too. Jesus saw the small man in the tree. He smiled because He knew how much the man wanted to see Him. Then, even though the small man had stolen from people, Jesus called him down, made friends with him and taught him about Father God.

The small man's name written backwards was SUEAHCCAZ. Write the letters the right way round to find out who he was:

_ _ _ _ _ _ _ _ _

No matter how TALL or small you are, or what bad things you might have done, God wants to be your Friend.

Growing up (2)

What would you like to be?

Doctor ☐

Famous inventor ☐

Teacher ☐

Zookeeper ☐

Footballer ☐

Mad scientist ☐

Pizza restaurant owner ☐

Actor ☐

Ice cream taster ☐

Circus performer ☐

Other (write details) _____

_____

What did Jesus learn to be as He grew up? Fill in the missing letters:

C _ _ _ _ _ _ r

What would you like to live in?
Unjumble the letters

varcana   _____

capes tinosta   _____

stacle   _____

gol binca   _____

naacl grabe   _____

wawgim   _____

cleapa   _____

reet shoue   _____

Other _____

_____

Answers on page 110

Football Mad ... or Not ...?

Do you like watching football on TV (tick a box)?

☐ A lot

☐ A bit

☐ Sometimes

☐ Depends what else is on

☐ Not really

☐ I'd rather eat a packet of pickled onion and raspberry flavour crisps

What's your favourite team?
Draw their badge/emblem.

Here are some of the Topz Gang's favourite football teams – can you find them in the word search?

Arsenal
Liverpool
Everton
Chelsea

Reading
Portsmouth
Sheffield
HollyHill

E	O	M	P	R	O	J	N	L	O	J	T
H	L	X	R	A	Y	P	O	I	Q	S	N
P	N	A	V	K	A	A	M	V	H	D	O
U	O	Y	N	E	X	A	F	E	X	E	T
R	U	R	L	E	E	T	F	R	K	L	R
I	W	D	T	S	S	F	N	P	U	V	E
O	I	E	L	S	I	R	O	O	Z	U	V
Z	S	E	Z	E	M	M	A	O	V	L	E
A	H	U	L	Z	E	O	S	L	I	V	P
C	T	D	Q	Z	C	T	U	G	F	H	U
R	E	A	D	I	N	G	U	T	A	U	P
L	L	I	H	Y	L	L	O	H	H	L	D

Answers on page 111

GUESS WHAT ...?
Competitive football was being played in England as far back as the thirteenth century. However, it was nearly wiped off the sports menu for good in 1314 when it was banned by King Edward II who thought it was far too dangerous!

Things I Like

What do you like most about ...?

Weekends _____

_____

_____

_____

School _____

_____

_____

_____

Your best friends _____

_____

_____

_____

Your bedroom _____

_____

_____

_____

_____

Your clothes _____

_____

_____

_____

Where you live _____

_____

_____

_____

Topz _____

_____

_____

_____

Being God's friend _____

_____

_____

_____

When you next get the chance to tell someone how amazing it is being God's friend, you can use what you've just written in the 'Being God's friend' space to help you.

Not-So-Great Stuff

What's your LEAST favourite ...?

 Vegetable _____

 Fruit _____

 Book _____

 Song _____

 Place _____

 Day of the week _____

 Film _____

 TV programme _____

 Lesson at school _____

Here's a prayer for you to say today. Add your own list of things you'd like to thank God for.

Dear Lord, there may be things I don't like, but there are plenty of things I do like, too.

Thank You for:

_____

_____

_____

_____

_____

I praise You for all You give me – today and every day. Amen.

Think about all the people who love you and take care of you, teach you and help you. Make a list of their names below and say thank you to them. As you thank each one, you can put a tick in their box.

_____	☐	_____	☐
_____	☐	_____	☐
_____	☐	_____	☐

Plan of the Park at Holly Hill

(Topz meet here lots.)

Toddlers' play area

Trees

Fountain

Picnic Area

Bench

Climbing frame

Big hedge

Round-about

Climbing ropes

Bench

Sand pit

Skate Park

Bench

Trees

Trees

Entrance

Design Your Very Own Ultimate Play Park

This is what MY ULTIMATE play park would look like:

More Ultimate Stuff ...

Plan your ULTIMATE Saturday meal menu:

Lie-in: Yes ☐   No ☐

For **BREAKFAST** I'm going to have _____

_____

For **ELEVENSES** I fancy _____

_____

For **LUNCH** I could really go for _____

_____

For a **TEATIME** snack I might have _____

_____

My one and only **ULTIMATE** choice for supper is:

_____

_____

Dave's been away for a week on an activity holiday. Here's a list of things he got up to. **Tick the boxes if you've ever done any of these:**

Horse riding ☐

Mountain biking ☐

Canoeing ☐

Raft building ☐

Raft racing ☐

Abseiling ☐

Orienteering ☐

What would you do on your ULTIMATE holiday?

_____

_____

If you have a stonking holiday, or go out and do something REALLY awesome, always remember to thank God for the fantastic time you've had.

If you could interview any famous person in the whole world, who would it be?

Here are the questions John would ask. Tick the ones you would ask too, and, as you do, imagine you're the famous person being interviewed and try to guess their answers ...

☐ What size shoes do you wear? _____

☐ What time do you get up at the weekend? _____

☐ Have you got a skateboard? _____

☐ If yes, do you skateboard to work/school? _____

☐ Do you know your times tables up to 12? _____

☐ If yes, prove it – what's 12 x 12? _____

☐ Do you have a sister and, if so, is she annoying? _____

☐ What's your favourite flavour ice cream?

☐ Have you ever invented anything REALLY interesting?

☐ If you had your very own spaceship, which planet would you visit first?

_____

☐ Do you wear a woolly hat in cold weather? _____

☐ If you had to decide between working in a pizza restaurant or in a shoe shop, which would you choose and why?

_____

_____

☐ If you could live anywhere in the whole world, where would it be?

_____

☐ How many books have you read and what was your favourite?

_____

_____

Over to You!

John would also like to interview YOU. Please fill in the answers to the following questions:

Do you ever wear a scarf?   Yes ☐ No ☐

Which do you prefer – thin chips or chunky chips?

Do you have any sisters?   Yes ☐ No ☐

If yes, have you ever hidden her/their
shoes when it's time to go to school? Yes ☐ No ☐

Do you know how to spell
MISCHIEVOUS?   Yes ☐ No ☐

If yes, prove it – cover it up above and then write it here

Have you ever met anyone
royal or famous?   Yes ☐ No ☐

Has anyone royal or famous
ever met you?   Yes ☐ No ☐

If you went into a library, what would you be more
interested in – books, CDs or DVDs?

If you had a magic carpet, which countries would you most like to visit?

_____

_____

If you had to swap ears with an animal, which animal's ears do you think would suit you best?

_____

How many pairs of socks do you own? _____

Do you manage to lose things easily? Yes ☐ No ☐

Thanks very much for your answers!

Is There an Author in You (1)?

Paul has an idea for a story. It's about a family of dragons who have to move house when their cave is discovered by a group of children on a school trip. If lots of people find out where they live, the dragons know they'll never get a minute's peace. During the night, they fly off to find a new cave, but the little dragon gets lost in the dark. It's some time, and quite a few adventures later, before he manages to find his family again ...

Can you help Paul write his story?

What names could he give each dragon?

Father Dragon _____

Mother Dragon _____

Little Dragon _____

What colour are the dragons? _____

How many teeth does each one have? _____

What do they like to eat? _____

Are they fire-breathing dragons?   Yes ☐   No ☐

Can you think of ONE idea for an adventure the little dragon might have before he finds his family?

_____

_____

_____

_____

_____

Paul has drawn the father and mother dragons. Add your drawing of the little dragon to his picture.

Is There an Author in You (2)?

If YOU were a NO 1 BESTSELLING AUTHOR, what would you write about in your next book ...?

Use the next few pages to help you start a story plan.

Main character (tick a box):

Boy ☐ Girl ☐ Creature ☐

Main character's name: _____

Age _____

Eye colour _____

Hair colour _____

Where does your main character live (tick a box)?

Near you   ☐

In another country   ☐

On a different planet   ☐

Other (describe) _____

_____

What does your main character like doing (tick a box)?

Playing sport ☐ Exploring jungles ☐

Watching TV ☐ Chasing baddies ☐

Other (describe) _____

_____

Will there be a baddy in your book? Yes ☐ No ☐

If yes, write his or her name: _____

What kind of adventure will your main character have?
Is he or she ...

Lost and trying to get home? ☐

In danger because they saw a bank robbery? ☐

Kidnapped by aliens and taken to another planet? ☐

Leading a mountain rescue? ☐

Trying to save the Prime Minister from baddies? ☐

A stowaway on a submarine? ☐

Is There an Author in You (3)?

Make a list of more possible ideas for your book here:

_____

_____

_____

_____

_____

The first few lines of a story are INCREDIBLY important. An author needs to grab a reader's interest straightaway. Paul's dragon story begins:

> *The cave was dark. Pitch dark. Under the boy's fingers, the rock walls felt damp and slimy. Suddenly he saw it! A flash of flame flickering in the blackness ...*

How might your story begin? Try and write the first few lines here:

_____

_____

_____

_____

_____

Paul's story is going to be called **'DRAGON DAWN'**.
When you've decided on an outline for YOUR story,
think about what you're going to call your book. Then
you can design a book cover for your masterpiece here,
including your title and your name as author:

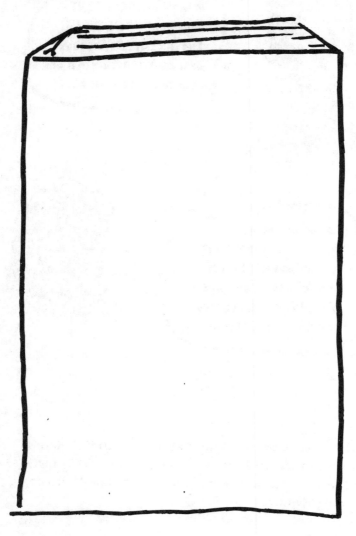

The Greatest Book of All

What's the GREATEST book of all? THE BIBLE! The 'GREATEST' because everything written in it has been inspired by God ...

'Book' because ... well ... it's a book! But it's divided into lots of smaller books, and was given to us by God so we could learn about Him ...

How much do you know about the Bible? Here's a quiz to test your knowledge of the GREATEST BOOK OF ALL. When you've finished, flip to page 111 to check your answers.

FILL IN THE MISSING LETTERS:

1 The Bible has two main sections. What are they called?

The O __ __ T __ __ __ __ __ __ __ __ __ &

The N __ __ T __ __ __ __ __ __ __ __

2 The life of Jesus is written about in four special books in the Bible. What are they known as?

The G __ __ __ __ __ __

3 Who wrote those four special books about Jesus?

M __ __ __ __ __ w, M __ __ k, L __ __e and J __ __n

4 Which Bible book tells the story of the creation of the universe?

The book of G __ __ __ __ __ __

5 What is the name of the very last book of the Bible?

The book of R __ __ __ __ __ __ __ __ __ __

6 We call the prayer Jesus taught to His disciples 'The Lord's Prayer'. How does it begin?

Our __ __ __ __ __ __

7 Jesus did incredible things such as turning water into wine and raising people from the dead. What do we call these amazing acts?

M __ __ __ __ __ __s

The Greatest Book of All
(continued)

Tick the right box:

1. What did God tell Noah to build to save himself and his family?

☐ A raft ☐ An ark ☐ A speedboat

2. When Jonah disobeyed God, he was swallowed by something huge. What was it?

☐ A huge lion ☐ A huge bear ☐ A huge fish

☐ A huge worm

3. Where was Jesus born?

☐ In a stable ☐ In a hospital ☐ At home

4. How many 'disciples' (special friends) did Jesus have?

☐ Ten ☐ Fifteen ☐ Twelve

5. What was Jesus' mother called?

☐ Mum ☐ Martha ☐ Mary

6. **What's the name of the very first man to be written about in the Bible?**

☐ Fred ☐ Barney ☐ Adam ☐ Joseph

7. **How many commandments does God give to His people in the book of Exodus?**

☐ Ten ☐ Fifteen ☐ Twenty

8. **When Jesus feeds 5,000 people, how many loaves of bread does He have to start with?**

☐ Fifty ☐ Five ☐ Five hundred

9. **Who did God save from a pit full of lions?**

☐ David Beckham ☐ Joshua ☐ Daniel

10. **What was the name of the king the wise men visited when they were looking for the newly born baby Jesus?**

☐ Nebuchadnezzar ☐ Herod ☐ Ahab

Answers on page 112.

GUESS WHAT ...?
There are 66 different books in the Bible and God wants to speak to us through all of them!

Benny's Barmy Wash Day

Benny recently answered some questions about personal care. Have a look at his answers, then flip over the page to answer the questions yourself.

How many times a day do you brush your teeth, and when?

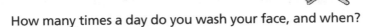

Not very often if I can help it.

How many times a day do you wash your face, and when?

Hate getting my face wet unless I'm swimming, so not often. (Also try to keep it dry in the shower.)

Do you wash your hands before you eat?

Only if I don't want the taste of my last meal to mix with the next.

How often do you have a bath or shower?

Depends on how hot and sweaty I get. If I've been really freezing all day, I don't bother.

How often do you get your hair cut?

Not often at all – I don't like the way the cut bits fall off and tickle my face. Haven't you noticed how long my fringe is?

How often do you cut/file your finger nails?

Whenever I start accidentally scratching my nose in my sleep. Sometimes I just bite them.

How often do you cut/bite your toe nails?

Eeew! That's just a disgusting question!

How often do you change your socks?

Once a week.

How often do you clean your ears?

Now you're just being silly ...

How would you rate your overall cleanliness?

Boring question, but I can eat six packets of crisps in one go without a break, and not even all the same flavour.

GUESS WHAT ...?
Until she broke them in a car accident in February 2009, Lee Redmond (USA), had not cut her nails since 1979, and they had reached a total length of 8.65 m (28 ft 4.5 in) as measured on the set of *Lo show dei record* in Madrid, Spain, on 23 February 2008.
The longest nail was the right thumb: 90 cm (2 ft 11 in).

Wash Day for You!

**Let's hope you're cleaner than Benny!
So here goes ...**

How many times a day do you brush your teeth,
and when?

_____

How many times a day do you wash your face, and when?

_____

Do you wash your hands before you eat?

_____

How often do you have a bath or shower?

_____

How often do you get your hair cut?

_____

How often do you cut/file/bite your finger nails?

_____

How often do you cut/file/bite your toe nails?

_____

How often do you change your socks?

_____

How often do you clean inside your ears?

_____

How would you rate your overall cleanliness?

_____

_____

Do you think you could teach Benny a bit about
personal care?

☐ Yes   ☐ No

Holiday Topz Tenz

Here are lists of ten things Dave, Benny and Josie would each take on holiday:

Dave's ten things:
Bike
Bike magazine
First aid kit
Radio
Torch
Map of holiday area
Tissues
Nuts & raisins (for energy while cycling a lot)
Frisbee
Pack of playing cards

Josie's ten things:
Sarah
Saucy, Sarah's cat (Sarah probably wouldn't go without her)
Notebook
Scrabble
Pens & crayons
Swingball
Favourite book
Umbrella
Diary
Board games

Benny's ten things:
Crisps
Biscuits
Sunglasses
Football
Skateboard
Chocolate (lots)
Hot chocolate powder
Cartons of custard
Bus timetable (you might need one)
Cheese

Here are lists of ten things they definitely would NOT take on holiday:

Dave's ten NOTS:
Stapler
Music magazine
Homework
Slippers
School shoes
Yoghurt maker
Tape measure
Potato peeler
Map of the world
Lawn mower

Benny's ten NOTS:
Mushroom-growing kit
Hairdryer (I'm on holiday – why would I wash my hair?)
Gooseberries
Sellotape
My school photo
School uniform
Maths text book
Boxing gloves
Tea bags
More than two pairs of socks

Josie's ten NOTS:
Alarm clock
Dictionary
Violin
Jigsaw puzzles
Best coat
Baked beans
Boring DVDs
Coat hangers
Calendar
Bucket

Your Holiday Topz Tenz

Your turn – what ten things would YOU take with you on holiday?

My ten things:

1 _____

2 _____

3 _____

4 _____

5 _____

6 _____

7 _____

8 _____

9 _____

10 _____

What ten things would you NOT take under any circumstances?

My ten NOTS:

1 _____

2 _____

3 _____

4 _____

5 _____

6 _____

7 _____

8 _____

9 _____

10 _____

Talking to God

At Sunday Club last week, Greg, the leader, asked everyone to write a prayer list – a list of people they'd like to pray for, and things they'd like to thank God for or ask for His help with.

Topz decided to write a joint list. That way they could pray their own prayers, and talk to God about the things their friends wanted to pray about, too.

TOPZ PRAYER LIST

1 Thank God that Paul found his glasses yesterday before someone sat on them.
2 John and Sarah's gran has broken her leg, so pray that it'll get better quickly.
3 Ask God to keep Sarah's neighbour, Mrs Allbright, safe when she leaves to visit her sister in Canada tomorrow.
4 Thank God for the brilliant cycling holiday Dave's just had.
5 There's a new boy in Benny's class at school, and Benny's worried he's being bullied. Ask God to take care of him and to help Benny be a good friend.
6 Danny's hurt his ankle. Pray that it will get strong again quickly so that he can run in the mini-marathon next month.
7 Ask God to stay close to Josie's adopted cousin because she needs to ask Him to be her best Friend.

Is there anything you need to talk to God about at the moment? Why not write your own prayer list here?

MY PRAYER LIST FOR _____

(Write today's date)

1 _____

_____

2 _____

_____

3 _____

_____

4 _____

_____

5 _____

When you pray, remember that God hears every word. He doesn't always say yes to the things we ask, but He always listens. And when you see Him answering one of your prayers – don't forget to say THANK YOU!

Food Glorious Food

1. If you could choose what to eat with your main meal, would you have ...?

☐ Chips ☐ Cooked vegetables ☐ Salad

☐ Chocolate

2. When you want a snack, do you reach for ...?

☐ Chocolate biscuits ☐ Piece of fruit ☐ Snails

☐ Piece of cake

3. When you eat fruit, do you ...?

☐ Eat it on its own ☐ Eat it with yoghurt

☐ Eat it with cream ☐ Play spit the pip

4. How often do you eat sweets ...?

☐ Every day ☐ Every midnight

☐ Twice a week ☐ Once a week

Flip to page 112 to check how healthy your choices are.

Here's a list of some healthy foods that are good for snacking on:

carrot sticks
apples
raisins
bananas

grapes
yoghurt
muesli bars
satsumas

Can you find them in the word search?

H	Z	S	C	H	D	O	W	Y	N	I	S
T	S	R	A	B	I	L	S	E	U	M	N
T	Y	Y	R	M	O	A	P	X	W	R	I
V	R	I	R	H	U	K	P	S	Y	S	S
K	G	K	O	S	O	S	D	P	A	W	I
U	L	C	T	H	E	N	T	N	L	B	A
A	T	Q	S	V	U	P	A	A	S	E	R
W	E	K	T	T	O	N	A	I	S	Y	S
O	L	V	I	E	A	M	U	R	W	R	A
Z	O	K	C	B	G	A	O	K	G	H	B
G	H	Z	K	Y	O	G	H	U	R	T	A
K	X	C	S	B	J	A	R	Q	B	C	H

Answers on page 112

It's fine to eat things like biscuits, sweets and cakes as long as you don't eat too many. If you do eat something sugary, try and remember to brush your teeth afterwards if you can – it'll help them last longer!

My Diary Profile

If you've read any of the *Topz Secret Diaries* or you use the *Topz* daily notes, you'll know quite a lot about the Topz Gang. But the Topz Gang don't know anything about YOU.

Here are some things they'd like to find out.

Please tick or write your answers ...

Have you ever sleep-walked? ☐ Yes ☐ No

Have you ever sleep-talked? ☐ Yes ☐ No

Have you ever walked more than five miles in one go when NOT asleep?

☐ Yes ☐ No

If yes, where did you walk from and to?

From _____ to_____

What's your favourite day of the week and why?

_____

_____

What's your favourite month of the year and why?

_____

_____

Have you ever written your name backwards and tried to pronounce it?

☐ Yes ☐ No

If you answered no, why not try it now?

Write your name backwards here: _____
Now try and say it ...

Did you manage to pronounce it? ☐ Yes ☐ No

Do you ever talk to animals as if you can understand each other?

☐ Yes ☐ No

Have you ever thought you'd make a good vet?

☐ Yes ☐ No

My Diary Profile (continued)

If you were camping, which would you prefer to find in your tent – a grasshopper or a spider? Why?

_____

_____

If you could meet a famous person from history, who would it be?

_____

If you were asked to be Prime Minister, what new laws would you make?

_____

_____

_____

_____

_____

As Prime Minister, would you keep your own name or would you choose a name that sounded quite grand, for example Cuthbert de Winkingslop-Smythe?

_____

If you could have apple crumble, apple and blackberry crumble or rhubarb crumble, which would you choose? (If you hate any kind of crumble, you need to go to the crumble appreciation school for crumble haters.)

Have you ever accidentally walked through a spider's web and got it stuck on your face?

'You' TV (1)!

Have you ever wanted your very own TV channel ...?
With your very own home-made programmes ...?
And your very own home-made advertisements ...?
All starring YOU ...?

Here's your chance to plan
YOUR IDEAL SATURDAY TV CHANNEL!

Channel name: (Helpful bit – the Topz Gang called
their channel 'TOPZ TV')

What would you like to be?

☐ Programme presenter   ☐ Programme
                                                  announcer

☐ Actor   ☐ Comedian

☐ Sports personality   ☐ Musician/singer

☐ Newsreader   ☐ Weather forecaster

☐ Interviewer   ☐ Sports commentator

(Helpful bit – Benny chose all of these and wanted to
be a TV cook, too ... Actually, perhaps that's not very
helpful at all ...)

What sort of programmes would you like to show on your TV channel (tick as many as you like)?

☐ Drama   ☐ Comedy

☐ Documentary   ☐ News and weather

☐ Sport   ☐ Music

☐ Chat show   ☐ Wildlife

☐ Reality TV   ☐ Games show/quiz

What would you like to see advertised?

☐ Food   ☐ Cinema films

☐ Washing powder   ☐ Clothes

☐ Music   ☐ Cars

☐ Toys/games   ☐ Books

☐ Toothpaste   ☐ Holidays

Other _____

'You' TV (2)!

Now think about the TV programmes you like to watch.
This will help you decide what you want your own
programmes to be about.

What are your favourite TV dramas?

_____

_____

_____

Your fave TV comedies?

_____

_____

_____

Favourite sport on TV?

_____

_____

_____

Fave ever documentary?

_____

_____

_____

Your favourite sort of music?

_____

_____

_____

Who would you have on your chat show?

_____

_____

_____

Favourite games/quiz shows?

_____

_____

_____

'You' TV (3)!

How it looks is up to you! Design a TV schedule for your Saturday TV channel!

Helpful bit – TOPZ TV's schedule for Saturday morning looks like this:

Saturday morning schedule for
TOPZ TV

9.00 — Breakfast programme including news, weather, interviews and music

10.00 — Comedy about children running a pizza delivery business

10.25 — Advertisements (Food)

10.30 — Sport – motorbike racing and tennis

11.25 — Advertisements (Toys)

11.30 — Games show with chocolate prizes

What does your Saturday TV channel schedule look like?
Make a list of programmes for morning and afternoon
below – don't forget to include programme start times.
Congratulations on being a TV channel planner!

Saturday schedule for

_____

(Write the name of your TV channel here)

MORNING

AFTERNOON

Topz Bible Challenge!

We've been learning some verses from the Bible by heart. Can you do the same? See if you can learn one verse a day for a whole week! Try and remember the Bible references, too (in brackets after each verse). Once a verse is learnt, you can put a tick in the box ...

Day 1: '... I am the LORD; no one who waits for my help will be disappointed.' (Isaiah 49 v 23)

Day 2: '... the Father himself loves you.' (John 16 v 27)

Day 3: 'The Lord is my helper; I will not be afraid.' (Hebrews 13 v 6)

Day 4: 'You are my God; teach me to do your will.' (Psalm 143 v 10)

☐

GUESS WHAT ...?
Remembering verses from the Bible can be very helpful. For example, if you're worried about something, keep saying the verse from Day 3. And if you want to thank God for something, you could say the verse from Day 7. The verses on these two pages teach us amazing things about our heavenly Father!

Day 5: 'Come near to God, and he will come near to you.' (James 4 v 8)

☐

Day 6: 'The LORD protects me ...' (Psalm 27 v 1)

☐

Day 7: 'Praise the LORD, my soul!' (Psalm 146 v 1)

☐

To help you learn and remember your verses, flip over the page to test yourself by trying to fill in the blanks. Only look back at this page once you've written in the missing words to check that you're right.

Topz Bible Challenge!

DO-IT-YOURSELF BIBLE VERSE TESTER

1 '... I am _ _ _   _ _ _ _ _; no one who

_ _ _ _ _ _ for my _ _ _ _ _ will be

_ _ _ _ _ _ _ _ _ _ _ _ _ _.'

(Isaiah 49 v _ _)

2 '... the _ _ _ _ _ _ _ himself _ _ _ _ _ _ you.'

(_ _ _ _ _ _ _ v 27)

3 'The _ _ _ _ _ is my _ _ _ _ _ _ _ _; I will not be

_ _ _ _ _ _ _.' (Hebrews _ _ v 6)

4 ' _ _ _ are my God; _ _ _ _ _ _ me to do

_ _ _ _ _ _ _ _ _.'

(_ _ _ _ _ _ _ _ _ v 10)

5 'Come _ _ _ _ _ to _ _ _ _, and he will come

_ _ _ _ _ to _ _ _ _.' (James _ _ _)

6 'The _ _ _ _ _ _ _ _ _ _ _ _ _ _ _ me ...'

(_ _ _ _ _ _ 27 v 1)

7 ' _ _ _ _ _ _ _ _ _ _ _ _ _ _ _, my soul!'

(Psalm _ _ _ _ _)

How did you do (tick a box)?

☐ Stonkingly

☐ Stonkingly-ish

☐ Need to learn them better!

More Topz Tenz

Paul recently got stranded in his dad's car when it ran out of petrol. While his dad walked to the nearest filling station, Paul had lots of time to think. Here are his TOPZ five things you might want to think about if YOU ever find yourself stuck in a car that's run out of petrol:

1 Picture what you'd look like with completely different colour hair and very large ears.

2 Picture what your best friend would look like with completely different colour hair and very large ears.

3 Design some unusual pizza toppings – for example, beetroot and cauliflower cheese, or peanuts and pickle.

4 Estimate how many potatoes might be used each year for:

(a) chips   (b) crisps   (c) roasts

5 Look at the inside of the car you're stranded in. What features could you add to make it more interesting?

Can you make Paul's list up to TOPZ ten with your own ideas for what to think about?

6 _____

_____

_____

7 _____

_____

_____

8 _____

_____

_____

9 _____

_____

_____

10 _____

_____

_____

Even More Topz Tenz

One place Paul's never been stranded is up in the air in a runaway hot air balloon. But, being Paul, he likes to be prepared for anything, so here is his TOPZ five list of things to do should it ever happen:

1 See if you can spot anything you recognise on the ground below you – for example your local swimming pool or the clothes of someone you know hanging on a washing line.

2 If anyone is having a barbecue, can you see what they are cooking?

3 Count the number of aeroplanes that fly past.

4 Whistle at passing birds and see if they notice you.

5 If you can't whistle, practise with favourite songs and TV programme theme tunes. For more of a challenge, make up some tunes of your own.

Can you make the list up to TOPZ ten so you've got
plenty to do if it should ever happen to you?

6 _____

_____

7 _____

_____

8 _____

_____

9 _____

_____

10 _____

_____

Can you think of anywhere else you might get
stranded where you would need plenty to do so as
not to get bored?

_____

_____

The Mostest!

Who would you ...?
(Write in your choices, including people you know and people you don't know but would really like to.)

... most like to play football with?

_____

... most like to borrow DVDs from?

_____

... most like to drive a train with?

_____

... most like to invent a new computer game with?

_____

... most like to cycle round the world with?

_____

... most like to build an igloo with?

_____

Who would you ...?

... most like to travel back in time with?

_____

... most like to travel forward in time with?

_____

... most like to hear singing in the bath?

_____

... most like to write a book with?

_____

... most like to see get a hair cut?

_____

... most like to ride an elephant with?

_____

More Mostest!

What would you ...?
(Imagine you could choose absolutely anything!)

... most like to do next weekend?

_____

... most like to watch on TV later?

_____

... most like to eat for breakfast tomorrow?

_____

... most like to see at the cinema?

_____

... most like to talk about with your class teacher?

_____

What would you ...?

... most like to give your best friend for Christmas?

_____

... most like to be given for your birthday?

_____

... most like to travel to school in?

_____

... most like to bury in a time capsule for people to discover in 100 years' time? (If you're not sure what a 'time capsule' is, ask someone you think will know.)

_____

... most like to thank God for right now?

_____

God's Way

When you live the way God wants you to, it makes Him happy and shows Him that you love Him and want to please Him. One way to live for God is to show His love to each other. Jesus told people to: 'Love your neighbour as you love yourself' (Mark 12 v 31).

Supposing there was someone new in your class at school? Look at the following list. Find and tick eight KIND things you could say to them to help them settle in. Put crosses beside the things it would be very UNKIND to say to anyone.

Would you like to sit beside me in class? ☐

Want me to show you where everything is? ☐

I can't be bothered to talk to you. I've got friends already. ☐

Want to share my crisps? ☐

Go away. We don't want you eating your lunch with us. ☐

Come and meet my friends. ☐

Leave me alone – you're weird! ☐

Want to come to our club at church? ☐

There's a new film on at the cinema. Why not come and see it with us? ☐

Why should I let you play with me? ☐

Shall we sit together on the school bus? ☐

I'm really pleased you've come to our school. ☐

More of God's Way

There are other ways of showing love, too. Lots of people need help – elderly or disabled people, for example, or people who aren't very well. Even very busy people sometimes need a helping hand.

A really good place to start giving some of your time to help out is at home. Find and tick eight things in the list below that would be helpful for you to do. Put crosses beside the things that wouldn't be helpful at all.

Don't bother to make your bed. ☐

Keep your bedroom clean and tidy. ☐

Offer to do the washing up after meals. ☐

Leave your towel in a heap on the floor after you've had a bath or shower. ☐

Do the vacuum cleaning. ☐

Put your toys and games away each time you finish playing with them. ☐

If your shoes are muddy, don't take them off when you go indoors. ☐

See if you can help with some of the cooking. ☐

Hang out washing to dry. ☐

Knock a jug of milk over in the fridge and
leave someone else to clear it up. ☐

Find out if your family's car needs washing,
then ask if a friend can help to wash it
with you. ☐

Help to carry grocery shopping in from the
car and put it away in cupboards. ☐

Every day, try and remember to ask if there's anything
you can do to help at home.

Benny's Guide to Powering Up Your Brain

Here they are! My EXCLUSIVE TOPZ tips for making the most of your BRAIN POWER! It's not just our bodies that need exercise. I reckon brains need a workout, too. So if you want a fully-powered, fandabulous brain like mine, read on and rev up the inside of your head!

TOPZ tip 1: Always eat breakfast. Your brain needs food to get it going in the morning just as much as you do.

TOPZ tip 2: Don't spend all your spare time watching TV. It stops you thinking about anything important and, let's face it, too much TV is just boring!

TOPZ tip 3: Get plenty of exercise. It'll help keep your brain alert.

TOPZ tip 4: Fresh air is good, too. Get outside whenever you can.

TOPZ tip 5: Get plenty of sleep. If you get really tired, your brain can't stay fully powered.

TOPZ tip 6:
Practise saying your times tables. Stonking exercise for brains! Puzzles are good, too, for example, word searches and crosswords.

Why not do a puzzle right now? Here's a list of things you can do to get your body moving and keep you fit. See if you can find them in the word search below and help your brain stay in tip-top condition, too!

BASKETBALL   CYCLING   DANCING
FOOTBALL   RUNNING   SKIPPING
SWIMMING   SKATING

B	A	S	K	E	T	B	A	L	L	F	G
R	U	N	N	I	N	G	G	S	F	O	N
R	B	S	V	Z	T	N	Z	K	F	O	I
G	N	I	M	M	I	W	S	A	J	T	P
L	S	B	B	L	S	C	K	T	U	B	P
G	N	I	C	N	A	D	S	I	X	A	I
U	F	Y	R	K	J	S	Y	N	Q	L	K
Q	C	E	B	E	W	I	C	G	S	L	S

Here's another brainteaser. Unmuddle the letters below to find five things from the opposite page that Benny recommends for powering up your brain.

psele _____

screixee _____

mitse ebtals _____

tasrkabfe _____

rehsf rai _____

Answers on page 113.

Is There a Designer in You (1)?

You *could* use these pages to spend ages designing something really dull like a cheese grater that won't grate your fingers when you get near the end of the lump of cheese, or a sandwich toaster that also puts the jam in doughnuts (yawn) – OR you *could* use them to design YOUR VERY OWN SPACESHIP!! So what are you waiting for? Here are some questions to help you come up with a super-snazzy, flying space machine that even someone who hates flying and isn't interested in outer space would be over the moon (ha! ha!) to have a ride in …

My spaceship is called (the name you give it might help you decide what it will look like):

_____

_____

Number of friends coming with you (the number of people travelling will affect how many 'rooms' you'll need on your ship):

_____

How long will you be gone for?

_____

What fun stuff to do would you build into your ship? For example, a games room with a table tennis table and trampoline would be brilliant, but if you put in a swimming pool as well, that would be totally awesome!

_____

_____

_____

How many different levels (floors) would there be?

_____

Will you have an escalator or stairs?

_____

Is There a Designer in You (2)?

What would you do on the moon?

Dave and Josie decided to design a spaceship together.
This is what they came up with:

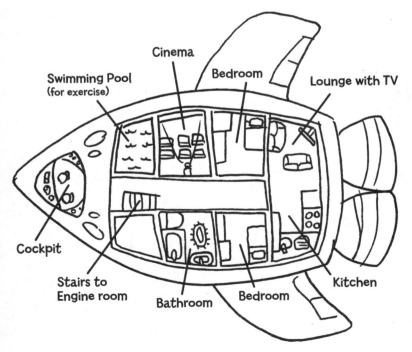

Cinema

Swimming Pool
(for exercise)

Bedroom

Lounge with TV

Cockpit

Stairs to
Engine room

Bathroom

Bedroom

Kitchen

OK, now you can design your very own spaceship!

Thank You, God, for the incredible universe You have
created. It doesn't just end with Earth, but goes on ...
and on ... and on ...

Favourite Bible Story

What's John's favourite?

Q John, do you have a favourite Bible story?
A Yes, definitely. The parable Jesus tells about the lost sheep.

Q Do you know where to find it in the Bible?
A Matthew 18 v 12–14 and Luke 15 v 3–7.

Q What happens?
A Jesus asks what a man would do if he owned 100 sheep and one of them got lost. He says that the man would leave the other 99 sheep to go and look for the one that was missing. However long it took, the man wouldn't stop searching until he found it – and then, wow, would he be happy!

Q Does this story teach you something about God?
A Yes! The man was really excited to find his missing sheep, which shows me God is really excited and happy every time someone new asks to be His friend. Jesus told this story to teach that God wants us ALL to be a part of His family. He doesn't want anyone to be like a 'lost sheep'.

John's prayer:

Thank You, Lord, for the awesome things Jesus teaches us about You – and for being the awesome God that You are. Amen.

What's your favourite?

Q Do you have a favourite Bible story?

_____

_____

Q Do you know where to find this story in the Bible?

_____

Q What happens?

_____

_____

_____

_____

Q Does this story teach you something about God?

_____

_____

Write a thank You prayer to God here:

_____

_____

_____

Are You Up for a Challenge?

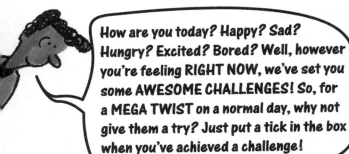

How are you today? Happy? Sad? Hungry? Excited? Bored? Well, however you're feeling RIGHT NOW, we've set you some AWESOME CHALLENGES! So, for a MEGA TWIST on a normal day, why not give them a try? Just put a tick in the box when you've achieved a challenge!

On your marks ... Get set ... GO!!

Stand on one leg for one minute without falling over. ☐

Stare at yourself in a mirror for one minute without blinking. ☐

Stare at someone else (for example, a brother, sister or best friend) for one minute without blinking AND without laughing. ☐

Think of three of your favourite crisp flavours. Can you spell them out loud BACKWARDS in one minute? ☐

Say, 'PAUL'S PERFECT PEANUT-FLAVOURED PORRIDGE' 35 times in one minute without getting all tongue-twisted. (Test: can someone else understand what you're saying on the 35th time?) ☐

Outside, bounce a ball up and down on the ground with ONLY ONE HAND 100 times in one minute without having to stop and start again. ☐

Outside, throw and catch a ball with only one hand WITHOUT DROPPING IT 50 times in one minute. ☐

Outside, throw and catch a ball with only one hand WITHOUT DROPPING IT 50 times in one minute, but this time STANDING ON ONLY ONE LEG. ☐

Don't worry if you can't do any of these challenges first time round. Just keep practising. When you can do them all, give yourself a **big tick HERE**:

The Best and the Worst

Imagine the whole of your life so far as a film. Which would be your choice of the most amazing moments EVER? A totally stonking birthday party or getting a puppy or scoring two goals in the same football match? If Benny's life so far was caught on camera, these would be his pick of the five best and five worst moments.

Benny's five best moments:

1 Deciding to live God's way and asking Him to be his friend!

2 Making up with Danny after they'd had a MASSIVE fallout over him getting picked for the Area Football Squad.

3 Seeing the grin on his dad's face when he told Benny he'd got a new job after he lost his old one.

4 When Greg asked him if he'd like to set up and run a magazine for Sunday Club.

5 When he stood up for one of his friends and helped stop them being bullied.

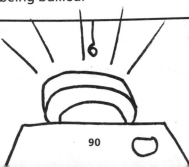

Benny's five worst moments:

1 The day he didn't get voted in as the new editor of his school magazine.

2 Being horrible to his mum and dad about having his little four-year-old cousin to stay when, as he found out, he's actually extremely cool.

3 Realising he was going to be stuck with Mr Mallory as his class teacher.

4 Finding out that one of his friends was being really badly bullied.

5 Getting bullied himself.

As you grow up, and all through your life, you'll find you have good days and bad days, brilliant times and times that aren't so easy. One of Benny's five best moments was when he asked God to be his friend. Now he knows that God's with him, not just when something fantastic happens but through the difficult moments, too. God promises to be with us ALWAYS.

Your Best and Worst

So, can you picture your life so far on film? Pick out five of YOUR very best moments and write them down here. Then, when you're much older you'll always be able to remind yourself of them and think, 'Yup, those were such good times!'

1 _____
_____

2 _____
_____

3 _____
_____

4 _____
_____

5 _____
_____

Write your five worst moments here:

1 _____

_____

2 _____

_____

3 _____

_____

4 _____

_____

5 _____

_____

If you're having a difficult time, talk to someone about it and don't forget to talk to God. He'll always be there to help you and comfort you. With God right beside you, you're never on your own.

Paul's Having a Party!

It's not just any old party, either. This is a top-of-the-range, megatastic, stonking, FANCY DRESS party, and all the Topz Gang are going. Below is a list of costumes. Write in the names of which Gang member you think would look good in which outfit.

Policeman/woman _____

Gorilla _____

Fireman/woman _____

Footballer _____

Banana _____

Dinosaur _____

Astronaut _____

Ice cream cone _____

Carrot _____

Bear _____

Clown _____

Robin Hood _____

Do you have any other ideas for fancy dress costumes for Topz? If yes, write them here:

_____

_____

If you were going to the party, what would you dress up as?

_____

Draw yourself in your costume with the Topz Gang dressed in the outfits you've picked for them to wear.

Crazy Football Moves!

Did you know that there's SO much more you can do with a football than just play football with it? Here are some CRAZY FOOTBALL MOVES we're going to be doing at my fancy dress party. Why not grab a friend and give them a try together?

Keepy-uppy, bouncing the ball from knee to knee. Time yourself for one minute. How many can you manage in one go without dropping the ball?

Hold the ball tightly between your knees. How many times can you jump up and down in one minute without letting it go?

Two of you lie on the floor and try to pass the ball backwards and forwards between you JUST USING YOUR FEET. How many times can you pass the ball without dropping it?

Number one stands with legs apart to form a 'goal'. Number two stands with back towards number one a short distance away, and tries to roll ball into 'goal' by kicking gently with heel of one foot.

Once you've mastered these moves, why not try and come up with some more of your own? Write down your ideas in the space below. When you've filled the page, see if you can organise a couple of CRAZY FOOTBALL TEAMS to take part in a CRAZY FOOTBALL MOVES EXTRAVAGANZA!

_____

_____

_____

_____

_____

_____

_____

_____

_____

_____

GUESS WHAT ...?
In January 2010, one man played keepy-uppy (using every bit of his body apart from his hands) non-stop for 30 miles, visiting all the Premier League stadiums in London. He started at 8 o'clock in the morning and didn't finish until around 9.45 at night!

How much do you know about where you live?

We're not talking about historical facts here. We're talking about the itsy-bitsy, nitty-gritty, day-to-day stuff about your local neighbourhood. How much do you know? Find out by seeing how many questions you can answer (correctly, of course ...).

How many people live in the houses next door to you (or in the nearest house if there isn't one right next door)?

_____

Do any cats live in the homes on your street? If yes, how many cats are there? (You can estimate if you don't know the exact number.)

_____

Do any hamsters live in the homes on your street? If yes, how many?

_____

What time does the postman usually arrive at your home (tick one)?

☐ Early morning ☐ Mid-morning

☐ Lunchtime ☐ Later

How many post boxes do
you pass on your way to school? _____

How many telephone boxes do
you pass on your way to school? _____

Do you walk across or drive over a pedestrian crossing on your way to school?

☐ Yes ☐ No

Can you see a shop from your bedroom window?

☐ Yes ☐ No

Is there a bus stop in your street?

☐ Yes ☐ No

How much do you know about where you live (continued)?

Do people walk their dogs past your home?

☐ Yes   ☐ No

If you live near a zoo, has an animal ever escaped and been found in your street?

☐ Yes   ☐ No   ☐ I don't live near a zoo

Has anyone famous ever lived in your neighbourhood? If yes, who are they and what are they famous for?

_____

What day are the dustbins emptied on your street?

_____

Does a mobile library van visit your neighbourhood or do you have a public library building?

_____

Has anyone royal (ie king, queen, princess or prince) ever visited your neighbourhood?

☐ Yes   ☐ No

Has a television series or film ever been made in your neighbourhood?

☐ Yes   ☐ No

If yes, what was it called?

_____

Does an ice cream van regularly visit your street?

☐ Yes   ☐ No

Is there a fish and chip shop within walking distance of your home?

☐ Yes   ☐ No

So, how well do you know your neighbourhood?

Write your score out of 18 here: _____

Home Sweet Home

However much or little you know about your neighbourhood, the most important thing is that you have a home to live in. And it's not just people who need somewhere to live ...

Here are some animals, birds, insects and fish, together with pictures of their 'homes'. Match each creature to its home by drawing a line between the two ...

Draw your own home here:

TOPZ PRAYER

Heavenly Father, I know there are people in the world who don't have anywhere comfortable to live, and others who have nowhere to live at all. Be with them, Lord, I pray, and please help me always to be so grateful for my own home. Amen.

Jesus said, 'There are many rooms in my Father's house, and I am going to prepare a place for you' (John 14 v 2). The AMAZING thing about being a friend of God's is that, as soon as you ask Him to forgive you for the wrong things you do and to come and share your life, you have a home with Him! Jesus, the Son of God Himself, makes everything ready for you.

What if ...?

Imagine being able to change places with someone for a whole day. Supposing you could see through their eyes and hear through their ears ... And supposing the someone you changed places with was ... A DOG ...!

If you were a dog ...

What would you like to be called?

_____

What would you want to eat for breakfast?

_____

Who would you choose to take you for a walk?

_____

What colour collar and lead would you want?

_____

Would you like cats? ☐ Yes ☐ No

Would you like other dogs? ☐ Yes ☐ No

Where would you want to sleep?

_____

Would you like having a bath? ☐ Yes ☐ No

Would you enjoy chasing a ball or other toy, or would you find it a bit of a waste of time but feel you should do it anyway because your owner seems to enjoy throwing things?

_____

How would you wake your owner up in the morning? Would you (tick one) ...:

Jump on their bed and lick their face? ☐

or

Bark loudly until the whole house is awake? ☐

or

Knock something over, such as a lamp, so that it makes a huge crash that no one could possibly sleep through? ☐

More Doggy Details

Would you be proud of your amazing sense of smell (dogs are famous for their sniffing out skills), or would you find it a bit annoying as some smells are just awful?

_____

What sort of things might you dream of doing – being a guide dog for the blind, for example, or winning the prize for being the dog who looks most like its owner?

_____

_____

If you did win a prize in a competition, what prize would you like to win? (Remember to think like a dog!)

_____

Would you like to have short hair, or hair that's very long and flops about when you run?

_____

If you were a police dog, what would you enjoy most (tick one)?

Riding in a police car? ☐

Chasing a bank robber really fast? ☐

Receiving a medal for being incredibly brave? ☐

Which of your friends would you choose to be a dog for a day with you?

_____

Draw yourself and your friend as the dogs you'd be HERE

Be Fruitful for God!

I suppose 'fruitful' is a bit of a funny word, but being 'fruitful' for God doesn't mean pretending to be a grapefruit or acting like a yoghurt! When you tell God you'd like to be one of His special friends, He sends His Holy Spirit to you to help you live your life His way. Letting the Holy Spirit begin to work inside you means AMAZING things can happen. God's Spirit will keep you close to your heavenly Father, and help you be kind and loving towards other people, and fabulously fruitful for Him!

The 'fruit' of the Spirit are written about in the Bible in the book of Galatians 5 v 22–23.

Can you find all these fruit in the word search …?

FAITHFULNESS	GOODNESS	HUMILITY
JOY	KINDNESS	LOVE
PATIENCE	PEACE	SELF-CONTROL

P	E	A	C	E	N	K	I	L	W	M	J
G	U	R	R	F	N	T	U	A	O	Y	O
K	I	N	D	N	E	S	S	D	V	V	Y
K	E	C	N	E	I	T	A	P	M	Z	E
F	A	I	T	H	F	U	L	N	E	S	S
L	O	R	T	N	O	C	F	L	E	S	O
G	O	O	D	N	E	S	S	C	J	P	U
D	D	B	P	Y	T	I	L	I	M	U	H

Answers on page 113.

There are other ways of keeping close to God, too. Crack the code below to find out what they are. When you've worked out the words, write them under the coded versions to remind yourself.

1* = a   1# = b   2* = c   2# = d   3* = e   3# = f etc:

10# 1* 6# 6* 5* 7# 4* to God.

6# 5* 10* 10# 3* 7# 5* 7# 4* to God.

10# 9# 11* 10* 10# 5* 7# 4* in God.

9# 3* 1* 2# 5* 7# 4* the Bible.

Check your code-cracking on page 113.

God's your Friend! He loves you and wants to be part of your life every day. So spend time with Him, just as you would with your other friends – because the best place to be is in GOD'S GANG!

Answers

Page 7
Benny's Potty Pets

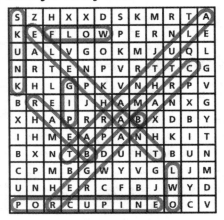

Page 16
What did Jesus learn to be as He grew up?

carpenter

Page 17
What would you like to live in?

caravan; space station; castle; log cabin; canal barge; wigwam; palace; tree house

Page 19
Football Mad ... or not

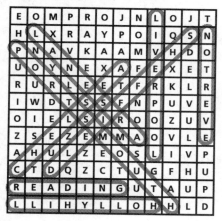

Page 39
1 The Old Testament & The New Testament
2 The Gospels
3 Matthew, Mark, Luke and John
4 The book of Genesis
5 The book of Revelation
6 Our Father
7 Miracles

Pages 40, 41

1 An ark
2 A huge fish
3 In a stable
4 Twelve
5 Mary
6 Adam
7 Ten
8 Five
9 Daniel
10 Herod

Page 52

Healthier choices are:
1 Salad or cooked vegetables
2 Piece of fruit
3 Eat it on its own or
  with yoghurt
4 Once or twice a week

Page 53
Food Glorious Food

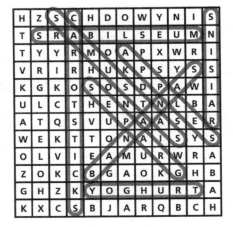

Page 81
Keeping Fit

B	A	S	K	E	T	B	A	L	L	F	G
R	U	N	N	I	N	G	G	S	F	O	N
R	B	S	V	Z	T	N	Z	K	F	O	I
G	N	I	M	M	I	W	S	A	J	T	P
L	S	B	B	L	S	C	K	T	U	B	P
G	N	I	C	N	A	D	S	I	X	A	I
U	F	Y	R	K	J	S	Y	N	Q	L	K
Q	C	E	B	E	W	I	C	G	S	L	S

sleep; exercise; times tables; breakfast; fresh air

Page 108
Fruit of the Spirit

P	E	A	C	E	N	K	I	L	W	M	J
G	U	R	R	F	N	T	U	A	O	Y	O
K	I	N	D	N	E	S	S	D	V	V	Y
K	E	C	N	E	I	T	A	P	M	Z	E
F	A	I	T	H	F	U	L	N	E	S	S
L	O	R	T	N	O	C	F	L	E	S	O
G	O	O	D	N	E	S	S	C	J	P	U
D	D	B	P	Y	T	I	L	I	M	U	H

Page 109
Coded words are:

Talking   Listening
Trusting   Reading

Give it your best

Dooooooooo

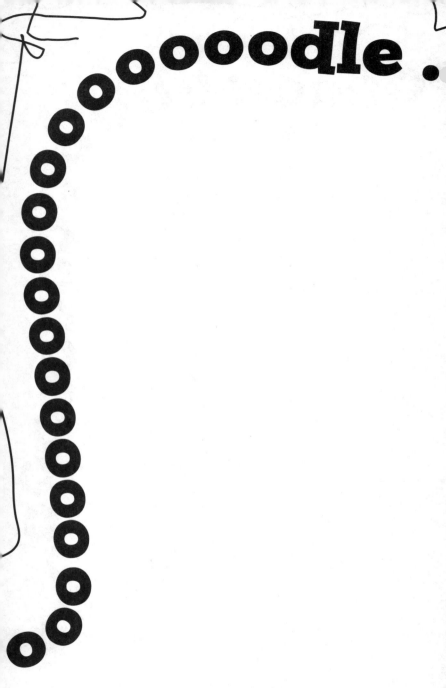

ooooodle.

Other Topz Secret Diaries for you to enjoy ...

Discover lots of stuff about yourself and God
Topz Secret Diaries: Just for Girls
ISBN: 978-1-85345-597-1

You can always talk to God
Dave's Dizzy Doodles
ISBN: 978-1-85345-552-0

Know God's help every day
Gruff and Saucy's Topz-turvy Tales
ISBN: 978-1-85345-553-7

Confidently step out in faith
Danny's Daring Days
ISBN: 978-1-85345-502-5

Become a stronger person
John's Jam-packed Jottings
ISBN: 978-1-85345-503-2

Keep your friendships strong
Paul's Potty Pages
ISBN: 978-1-85345-456-1

You can show God's love to others
Josie's Jazzy Journal
ISBN: 978-1-85345-457-8

Christians needn't be boring
Benny's Barmy Bits
ISBN: 978-1-85345-431-8

You are special to God
Sarah's Secret Scribblings
ISBN: 978-1-85345-432-5

For current prices visit **www.cwr.org.uk/store**
Available online or from your local Christian bookshop

Let the Topz Gang guide you through the Bible

With the *Topz Guide to the Bible* you'll discover the exciting story of the Old Testament from start to finish, learn what the world was like in Jesus' day, and find out what each book in the Bible is about.

And the Topz Gang will make it fun all the way with their usual blend of colourful illustrations, cartoons, word games, puzzles and lively writing. This is the perfect way for 7- to 11-year-olds to get to know their Bibles.

**ISBN:
978-1-85345-313-7**

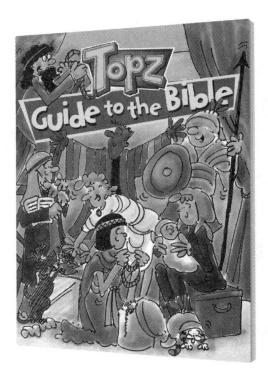

If you liked this book, you'll love our *Topz* daily Bible-reading notes!

An exciting, day-by-day look at the Bible for children aged from 7 to 11. As well as simple prayers and Bible readings every day, each issue includes word games, puzzles, cartoons and contributions from readers. Fun and colourful, *Topz* will help you get to know God.

ISSN: 0967-1307

£14.95 UK annual subscription (6 issues, bimonthly, includes p&p)

£2.75 each (single copies, published bimonthly)

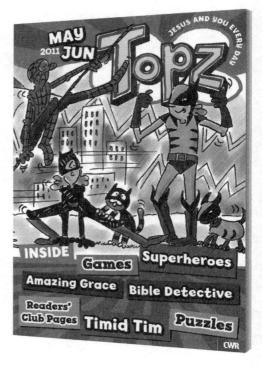

Topz for New Christians

Thirty days of Bible notes to help you find faith in Jesus and have fun exploring your new life with Him.

ISBN: 978-1-85345-104-1

**Available online (www.cwr.org.uk/store)
or from your local Christian bookshop.**